Look and Find

Alice
in
Wonderland

The Mad Hatter • The White Rabbit

The Cheshire Cat • The Caterpillar

The Queen of Hearts • And more!

Illustrated by Ernie Colon

Illustration script development by Jane Jerrard

Louis Weber, C.E.O.
Publications International, Ltd.
7373 North Cicero Avenue
Lincolnwood, Illinois 60646

Manufactured in the U.S.A.

8 7 6 5 4 3 2 1

ISBN 0-7853-0065-1

PUBLICATIONS INTERNATIONAL, LTD.

"Oh dear! Oh dear! I shall be too late!" said the White Rabbit as he hurried by.

And so begins Alice's great adventure, as she follows this most peculiar rabbit down his most peculiar hole. How far down will she fall?

Look for Alice and the White Rabbit. Then find these items that the White Rabbit has lost.

Alice

A top hat

The White Rabbit

A pocket watch

A morning coat

An umbrella

A handkerchief

A pair of shoes

Alice's adventures in Wonderland are off to a crazy start when she drinks from a bottle and becomes quite small. Next, she eats a piece of cake that makes her grow nine feet tall. Finally, after shrinking again, Alice finds herself swimming in a pool of her own tears! And she has plenty of company.

Can you find Alice and all of these animals and things she has encountered in Wonderland so far?

Alice

This mouse

This bottle

DRINK ME

This cake

EAT ME

A dodo

This table

An eaglet

A gold key

The White Rabbit has returned home to quite a surprise. Alice, after drinking from another magical little bottle, is as big as a house. Unfortunately, she's inside the White Rabbit's house, and she can't get out!

Look for these things and animals around the White Rabbit's house, including the bottle of liquid that made Alice grow and the magic cakes to help Alice shrink again.

The magic cakes

The White Rabbit

Bill the Lizard

The brass houseplate

The White Rabbit's gloves

The bottle

Pat the Gardener

The White Rabbit's fan

A normal, everyday lawn can sure look big when you're only three inches tall. Alice has gone through more remarkable changes, and now she can see eye-to-eye with a caterpillar.

Luckily, the caterpillar knows how Alice can return to her normal height. Can you find Alice, the caterpillar, and these other three-inch-tall items?

Alice

The caterpillar

A field mouse

This centipede

This butterfly

A four-leaf clover

A grasshopper

A hummingbird

"Achoo!" What else can you say when you enter the Duchess's peppery kitchen?

Alice's next visit in Wonderland is to the Duchess's house. Here she meets the hot-tempered Duchess, a baby who turns out to be a pig, and the disappearing Cheshire Cat.

Can you find them all, along with these other characters Alice meets at the Duchess's house?

Alice

The pig

The Duchess

The Cook

The Frog Footman

The Fish Footman

The Cheshire Cat

Alice next comes upon a most unusual tea party. The long table is set for tea, so she takes a seat.

"No room! No room!" cry the Mad Hatter and the March Hare.

"There's plenty of room!" says Alice indignantly, for places are set for many guests.

Can you find these things that are scattered around the Mad Tea Party?

This china teapot

This cup and saucer

A jar of marmalade

This fancy cake

This creamer

This sugar bowl

A silver tray

Things just keep getting curiouser and curiouser as Alice joins the Queen of Hearts's croquet game.

"Off with their heads!" is the Queen's favorite sentence, so let's hope Alice manages to keep hers as she plays this most curious game.

Can you find Alice, the Queen of Hearts, and these other cards in the Queen's garden?

The Queen of Hearts

Alice

The King of Hearts

The two of hearts

The five of spades

The jack of diamonds

The three of clubs

The ten of spades

Have you ever seen a Gryphon or a Mock Turtle? Alice meets these two unusual creatures after the Queen's croquet game. After listening to the Mock Turtle's sad tale, she learns an exciting new dance called the Lobster Quadrille.

Can you find Alice, the Gryphon, the Mock Turtle, and these dancing lobsters in this seaside scene?

Alice

The Gryphon

The Mock Turtle

Bobby Lobster

Rudolph Lobsterev

Ginger Lobsters

Red Nasty

Juanita Lobsterita

Alice's adventures in Wonderland end with the trial of the Knave of Hearts, who stands accused of stealing some tarts. Alice arrives to find some familiar faces in the courtroom. The question is, can you find them?

Alice

The Knave of Hearts

The Mad Hatter

The White Rabbit

The Queen of Hearts

The King of Hearts

Bill the Lizard

The Gryphon

The Duchess's Cook

LONG ARM OF THE LAW

RECESS 10:30 HOMEROOM 8:30

"FIRST THE SENTENCE, THEN THE VERDICT"

EYEWITNESS

TODAY'S TRIAL KNAVE OF HEARTS FOR TART THEFT

SMALL CLAIMS COURT

EXHIBIT A

BEE

COURT-SHIP

Go back to the Rabbit Hole, where Alice first "dropped in" on Wonderland. Can you find these other "falling" things?

- ☐ A falling "star"
- ☐ "Knight" fall
- ☐ London Bridge falling down
- ☐ A fallen cake
- ☐ Someone falling asleep
- ☐ A boxer "taking a fall"
- ☐ People "falling in love"

Return to the pool where Alice is swimming in her own tears. Can you find these famous criers?

- ☐ A crocodile crying "crocodile tears"
- ☐ A town crier
- ☐ A crybaby
- ☐ The boy who cried wolf
- ☐ A crying ghost
- ☐ The mother of the bride
- ☐ Someone crying over spilt milk

Find your way back to the White Rabbit's house, where Alice has grown too big for her britches. Can you spot these other "big" items?

- ☐ Big "time"
- ☐ A big wheel
- ☐ A big wig
- ☐ A big "top"
- ☐ Big Ben
- ☐ Big "game"
- ☐ A big dipper

Backtrack to the scene where Alice is as tall as a caterpillar. Can you find these silly insect characters?

- ☐ A firebug
- ☐ A bee in a bonnet
- ☐ A "June" bug
- ☐ A bookworm
- ☐ A Queen Bee
- ☐ A daddy long-legs spider
- ☐ Two ladybugs
- ☐ A "house" fly
- ☐ A lightning bug